First published in North
America by Annick Press 2002
Text © 2001 Meg Clibbon
Illustrations © 2001 Lucy Clibbon
Originally published by Zero To Ten Limited
(a member of the Evans Publishing Group)
© Zero To Ten Limited 2001

Cataloging in Publication Data
Clibbon, Meg
Imagine you're a pirate
North American edition
(Imagine this! series)
ISBN 1-55037-741-8 (bound).--ISBN 1-55037-740-X (pbk.)
1. Pirates--Juvenile literature. I. Clibbon, Lucy II. Title.
III. Clibbon, Meg. Imagine this! series.
G535.C55 2002   j364.1'64   C2002-900423-3

Distributed in Canada and the U.S.A. by Firefly Books Ltd.

www.annickpress.com

Printed in Hong Kong.

Imagine you're a
Pirate!

Peg Leg Meg
(also known as Meg Clibbon)

Meg gave up being a pirate two years ago and
now lives the life of a landlubber with her husband, John.
She has a gypsy caravan where she writes about
the secrets of the sea and a dog whom she is training
to look for treasure, but so far he has only found bones.
She tries to follow the pirates' code but finds it
very difficult (especially rule #6).

Lucy Blackheart
(also known as Lucy Clibbon)

Lucy lives in an enchanting faraway land where
she paints pictures about her favorite things.
She has often imagined having exciting adventures and
discovering treasure islands and meeting mermaids.
However, she would much rather stay at home painting
about the life of a pirate than suffer the hardships of
being a real one herself.

We dedicate this book to Simona – a real treasure!

What is a pirate?

Definition:
a robber who attacks
other ships at sea.

What do pirates look like?

There are some pirates who are big and strong and bold.

There are some pirates who are tall and thin and cunning.

Pirates can come in many different shapes and sizes, but ...
all pirates are very, very wicked.

Becoming a pirate

You can become a pirate by running away from home with all your things tied up in a spotty hanky. You have to walk to the nearest port and become a cabin boy or girl on a pirate ship. Then you have to learn how to be very, very wicked. This takes a long time and gets a bit boring after a while, so most people prefer to stay at home and watch a bit of television with a delicious supper!

The Pirate Code

1 Never be kind to children (especially the cabin boy or girl).
2 Never be kind to mermaids.
3 Never be kind to anyone.
4 Always look fierce.
5 Always carry a cutlass.
6 Always obey the captain.

The pirate motto:

Rob or rot!

What do pirates wear?

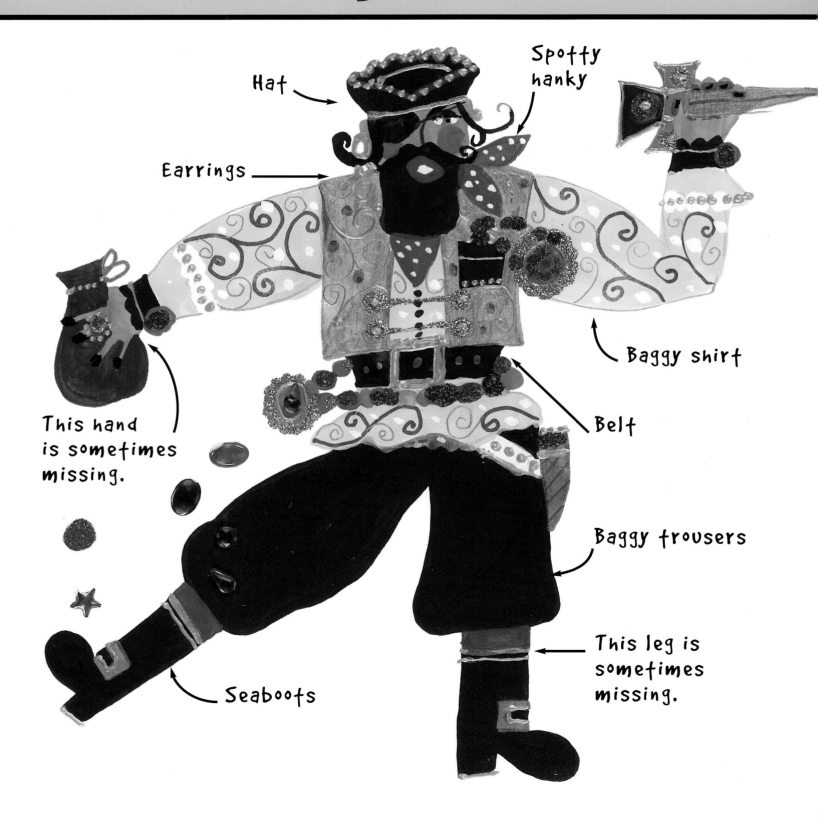

Hat

Spotty hanky

Earrings

Baggy shirt

This hand is sometimes missing.

Belt

Baggy trousers

Seaboots

This leg is sometimes missing.

Equipment and accessories

In order to be a pirate you will need some of the following equipment…

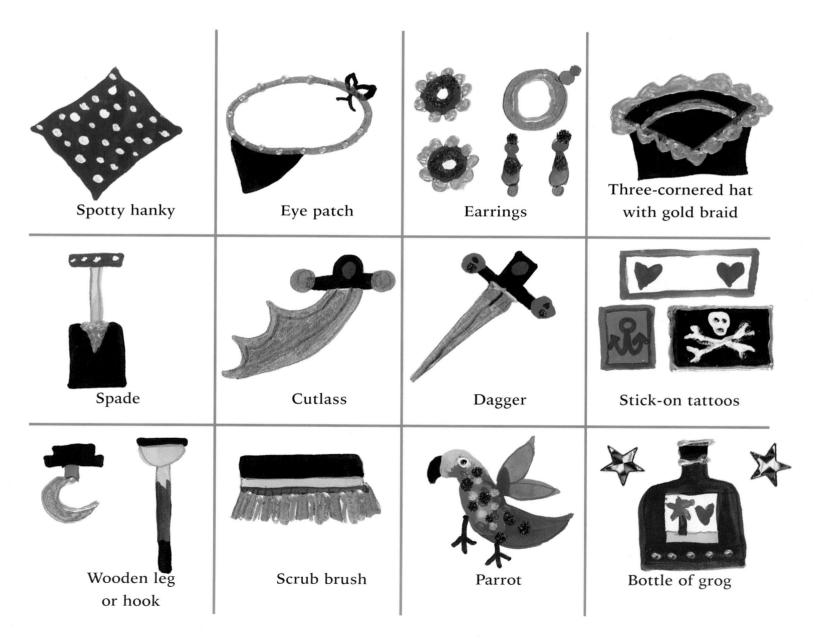

Spotty hanky

Eye patch

Earrings

Three-cornered hat with gold braid

Spade

Cutlass

Dagger

Stick-on tattoos

Wooden leg or hook

Scrub brush

Parrot

Bottle of grog

Where do pirates work?

Pirates sail the Seven Seas looking for ships to rob.
Nobody really knows where the Seven Seas are.
There are several oceans—Pacific, Atlantic, Arctic, Indian,
and Antarctic—and many seas, such as the Irish Sea,
the Caribbean, the Mediterranean, and the China Sea,
but only pirates can find the Seven Seas.

The Seven Seas have mermaids and sunken vessels
and coral reefs and treasure islands, but you have to be
a pirate to get there.
At the bottom of the Seven Seas is something called
Davy Jones's locker. Pirates say that when they die or
get killed and are thrown overboard, they float
down to Davy Jones's locker and live
with the mermaids.

Scattered around the Seven Seas are
many treasure islands. When the pirates have worked out
which one is which, they set sail. This is not always very easy
because they encounter various difficulties on the way, such as
sea monsters, typhoons, and marauding buccaneers or mutineers on
board ship, and they often run out of grog.
The only thing that keeps them going is the hope that they might
meet some friendly mermaids. Mermaids have bodies like women and
tails like fish and they comb their seaweed green hair
with shells.

They are very beautiful but not very reliable and sometimes
end up putting the pirates off their job of searching for treasure.
Eventually the pirates find the treasure islands and the treasure.
Treasure is always jewels, or pieces of eight, or doubloons,
or Spanish gold, and it is kept in big treasure chests buried
in sand or caverns.

The Jolly Roger

You always know which is a pirate ship because it will be
flying the pirates' flag called the **Jolly Roger**. It is a black flag with
a white skull and crossed thigh bones on it, sometimes known
as the skull and crossbones. When you see this flag, you
get very, very frightened.

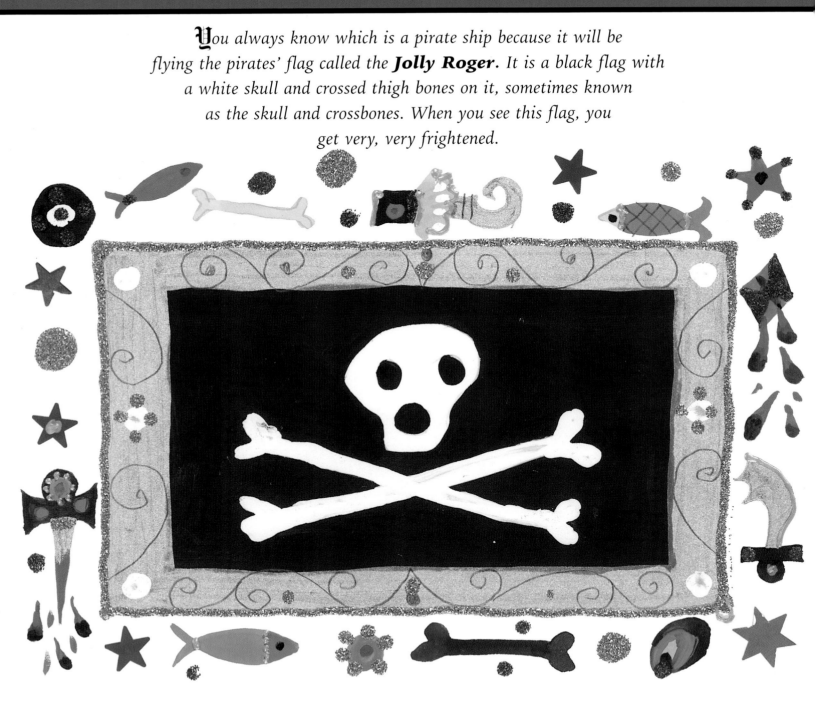

Pirates never buy their own ships. They always steal other people's ships, so they often have pretty names such as ...

Saucy Sue

Lovely Lady

PRETTY PEGGY

Hispaniola

The ship and her captain

Imagine you are the captain of a real pirate ship. Think of a really wicked name for the ship and then draw a picture of what you'd like her to look like.

The only friends that pirates really have are parrots, because they sit on their shoulders and say funny things like, "Who's a pretty boy then?"

Black Revenge

Food and drink

Pirates are at sea for most of the time, so they cannot get very much fresh food. They do not get enough vitamins, so they get spots and scurvy. Scurvy is a nasty disease you get when you don't eat the right sort of food.

They eat lots of fish.

They eat lots of ship's biscuits, which get very maggoty.

They also drink lots of rum, or grog, which they like better than the water kept in barrels on deck.

WATER

WATER

When pirates have been drinking, they like nothing better than to sing a jolly pirate song. Here are two of their favorites.

Fifteen men on a dead man's chest
Yo ho ho and a bottle of rum
Drink and the devil had done for the rest
Yo ho ho and a bottle of rum.

What shall we do with the drunken pirate?
What shall we do with the drunken pirate?
What shall we do with the drunken pirate?
Early in the morning.

Pirates behaving badly

When pirates disobey the pirate captain, they can be cruelly punished in a number of ways ...

Flogging

The captain ties them to the mast and hits them with a nasty whip with long strands, called a cat-o'-nine-tails, until they are very sorry. Then he throws salt water onto their wounds. Oh, dear!

Scrubbing the deck

(This is the worst punishment.) They have to pull up a bucket of salty water from the sea, get down on hands and knees with a scrub brush, and scrub the entire deck with a constant circular motion until it is clean. Oh, dear! Oh, dear!

Walking the plank

When pirates capture other ships, they sometimes make their captives walk the plank. They tie a plank to the deck so that it sticks out over the sea. Then they make their victims walk to the end so that they fall in –
S P L A S H !

oh, dear! oh, help!

Wanted
Black-Hearted Bill
For evil deeds on the High Seas
Description: Black greasy hair, dirty teeth,
snarling lips, scar on chin, black mustache
Beware
Do not approach this pirate

Pirate language

Pirate words

treasure

skull and crossbones

deck   cabin   cutlass

telescope

eyeglass   maroon   lagoon   crew

seaboots   *doubloon*   *ocean*

compass   **landlubber**

coral reef

musket

If you don't know these words, you could look them up in the dictionary!

Famous pirates in books

Captain Hook

Captain Hook is the pirate in J.M. Barrie's book Peter Pan. *He had a hook because Peter Pan chopped off his hand with a sword during a fight.*

A passing crocodile had eaten the hand and found it to be so delicious that from then on he chased after Captain Hook in order to eat the rest of him. Fortunately, he had also swallowed an alarm clock, so Captain Hook always knew when the crocodile was coming.

Tick-tock

Long John Silver

Long John Silver is the pirate in Treasure Island *by R.L. Stevenson. He pretended to be an honest man on board a ship called the* Hispaniola, *which was searching for treasure, but really he was the head of a pirate gang who were after the treasure for themselves. Long John Silver had a wooden leg instead of a real one and a parrot which perched on his shoulder screeching,*

"Pieces of eight ... pieces of eight."

Two real pirates

Blackbeard

This wicked pirate started off with a very ordinary name, Edward Teach, and a very ordinary job of being a seaman. But in 1716 he became a pirate and grew a huge jet-black beard. He liked his beard so much that he plaited it and tied ribbons in it.

He liked being wicked so much that he wore three pairs of pistols, a cutlass, lots of daggers, and slow-burning fuses under his hat. It didn't do him any good, though, because he was hunted down and killed, which was probably a good thing.

Grace O'Malley

Grace O'Malley, the Pirate Queen of Connaught, was born hundreds of years ago when all women wore long frocks. Grace became a pirate so that she could wear pirate clothes and sail the Seven Seas. She was very good at it and made lots of money robbing other ships.

Unfortunately, some of the ships belonged to Queen Elizabeth I of England. Grace had to go to England to have her head chopped off, but, amazingly, Queen Elizabeth seemed to like Grace and gave her a lace handkerchief instead! Perhaps she wished she could have been a pirate too, instead of just an ordinary queen.

Things to do

Message in a bottle

Imagine that you have been captured by pirates and then marooned on a deserted island. You have a few essential supplies, such as a box of ship's biscuits and a bottle of grog, but you need to be rescued. Write a message which can be sealed up in a bottle and thrown into the sea.

Wanted Poster

*Make your own **Wanted** poster by dressing your best friend up as a pirate (use old curtain rings for earrings, spotty hanky wrapped around head, false beard on chin, etc.) and drawing a picture of him or her. Try inventing your own "olde worlde" style of writing for the words on the poster.*

Pirates' treasure map

To help them find treasure, pirates always have a treasure map, which is usually very, very old and difficult to follow. It is dipped in tea and torn around the edges, then rolled up and fastened with ribbon. Can you make your own treasure map?

Pirates' grog

This is a drink which pirates make to keep them warm on deck. It also has plenty of vitamin C in it, which stops them from getting scurvy.

For each pirate you need:
- lemon
- tablespoon of brown sugar
- pinch of powdered ginger
- jug of hot water

Directions

1 Cut the lemon in half and squeeze out the juice.

2 Put juice in jug and add sugar and ginger.

3 Add hot water and stir well.